Bluebird Finds a Home

story by Ryan Jacobson and illustrations by Joel Seibel

Adventure Publications, Inc.
Cambridge, MN

Dedication

For Jonah and Lucas,
You make my world a better place.

—Ryan Jacobson

Nest box photo (pg. 29) by Stan Tekiela
Cover and book design by Jonathan Norberg
Edited by Brett Ortler

10 9 8 7 6 5 4 3 2 1

Copyright 2011 by Ryan Jacobson and Joel Seibel
Published by Adventure Publications, Inc.
820 Cleveland St. S
Cambridge, MN 55008
1-800-678-7006
www.adventurepublications.net

ISBN-13: 978-1-59193-311-3
ISBN-10: 1-59193-311-0

Meet the Nature Squad

A rumble echoed through the woods.

"That sounds like thunder," said Mr. Rivers.

Not thunder. B.B. was hungry. The bear's stomach groaned as he scanned the clearing.

Workers cut down all the dead trees, thought the bear. *No big deal. At least they left plenty of garbage to eat.*

B.B. didn't see any food scraps though. Instead, he found his Nature Squad buddies picking up the litter.

Kingston fluttered onto a stump beside the bear. "Where have you been? I ordered everyone to help clean this mess."

B.B. didn't have a good excuse. He had been showing the workers even more dead trees to chop. After all, the workers fed him such delicious snacks.

"Litter can make animals sick," said Mr. Rivers, "or cause a forest fire."

"But where's the food?" whined B.B.

Mr. Rivers tapped his bag. "In here. You know our rule. Humans should never feed wild animals, and wild animals should never eat human food."

Sheldon added, "You shouldn't eat their food, and they shouldn't cut down so many trees."

"The workers are only taking dead trees," B.B. protested. "What's the harm in that?"

"I'll tell you," chimed a new voice. "My name's Skylar, and I'm looking for a home. We bluebirds live in dead trees, but I can't find one."

"Maybe we can help," offered Kingston.

"You would do that?" chirped the bluebird.

"We're the Nature Squad. We'll find a dead tree in no time."

B.B. remembered the old trees he had shown the workers. *If Skylar finds those trees, he'll move in. The workers won't come back, and I'll never get any leftovers. I can't let that happen.*

That gave B.B. an idea. "I'll do it," he offered. "I'll find that bluebird a house."

"A fine plan," Kingston declared.

The bear smiled. "I know just the place."

He led Skylar toward Baker's Pond. "This is it," said B.B., pointing toward a tall tree trunk.

"It's perfect!" the bluebird exclaimed.

"There's just one thing," noted B.B. "You'll be living with wood ducks."

"Come in," said Woodra. "You're welcome here."

Skylar glided into his new home. The nest was lined with feathers, perfect for relaxing.

My search is over, thought the bluebird. He closed his eyes and slept.

The very next day, Woodra announced, "It's time for you to go, dear." She nudged him toward the hole.

"What do you mean?" asked Skylar.

"My ducklings jump out a day after hatching. You should too." She nudged him again, harder this time.

Skylar tumbled out of the tree, landing with a thud.

"Sorry dear," called Woodra. "I thought you could fly."

"I can," the bluebird pouted. "I'm not used to being pushed!"

He flapped his wings and soared skyward. He needed to find B.B.

"No problem," said the bear. "I have a backup plan."

He escorted his friend to a tree in the valley. "There's a beautiful nest up there. Some blue jays offered to share it."

Skylar fluttered to the nest.

"Make yourself at home," said Papa Jay.

Skylar nestled into a soft corner and closed his eyes. He could get used to living under the open sky.

Skylar's eyes shot open. He pressed his wings against his ears. "What is that terrible noise?"

"Jay! Jay! Jay!" his nest mates sang. "What noise?"

"Do you shout like that a lot?" the bluebird asked.

"All day," replied Papa Jay.

Skylar sighed. "I can't live here." He thanked the blue jays and flew back to B.B.

"Don't worry," offered the bear. "I have one more idea."

He brought Skylar to see his turtle friend. "You can live in Sheldon's shell," B.B. declared.

The bluebird peeked inside. "I can't do it," he yelled. "It smells like lily pads in there!"

"And it's kind of crowded," added Sheldon.

Skylar dropped onto the grass. "I'll never find a home," he cried.

A rumble filled the air.

"And now it's going to rain!"

B.B. knew it wouldn't rain. He was hungry again. *Is eating human food more important than finding Skylar a nest?* he wondered.

"I'll have to try a different forest," whimpered the bluebird.

"No," B.B. decided. "Come with me."

He gathered the Nature Squad and led Skylar to a gray corner of the woods.

"I was saving these trees for the workers," said the bear. "You can live here instead."

Skylar chirped excitedly. "Thank you, B.B. It's a dream come true!"

"What about the humans?" asked Red. "Won't they take these trees?"

"I'll tell them they've cut enough," said B.B. "If they chop down all the dead trees, the bluebirds, raccoons and other animals won't have a place to live."

"I'll come too," Mr. Rivers volunteered. "Someone should tell them not to feed the bears."

"So much damage has already been done," noted Skylar. "Is there anything we can do?"

Mr. Rivers smiled hopefully. "In fact, there is."

He showed the animals how to build
nest boxes—little homes for birds. Then
together, they spent the week making
their forest a better place.

How to Build a Nest Box*

Materials needed:

untreated, weather-resistant wood (such as cedar):
- 1" x 6" x 4' board
- 1" x 10" x 10½" board (the roof)

20–25 nails, 2 screws, 1 double-headed nail

tools: saw, ruler, pencil, hammer, drill, chisel

Building instructions:

1. Divide the 1" x 6" x 4' board into pieces, as shown below.

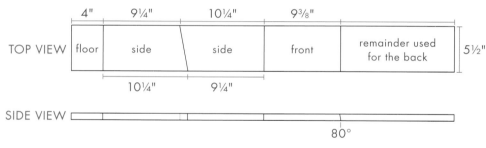

2. With your drill and chisel, create a 1½" hole on the front board. Center the hole between the side edges, about 6½" from the bottom.

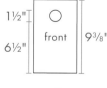

3. Cut the corners off the floor piece, about ¼" from the tips, to allow for drainage.

* **These instructions are intended for grown-ups.**

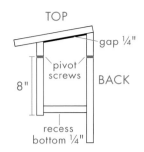

TOP

gap ¼"

pivot screws

8"

BACK

recess bottom ¼"

4. Nail together the front, back, bottom, roof and left side. The top piece should be flush with the back of the nest box and centered over the side edges. Take special care to leave a ¼" gap between the roof and each side piece. This will allow for ventilation.

5. Put the right side into place and screw pivot points through the front and back pieces (into the side piece), about eight inches above the floor. This should hold the right side into place, while allowing you to easily flip it open as needed.

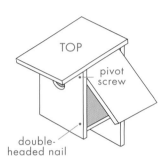

TOP

pivot screw

double-headed nail

6. Drill a hole through the front piece (into the side piece) about two inches above the floor. Slide a double-headed nail into the hole to hold the door closed.

Mounting instructions:

1. Choose an open area within 100' of trees and well away from any buildings.

2. Mount the nest box 4–6' above ground, preferably on a post or pole facing a nearby tree or shrub. Some experts suggest facing the nest box east or north.

3. To keep predators away, create a funnel-shaped metal (such as tin) barrier and place it around the mounting surface, approximately 8" below the nest box.

Building a Better World:
Conservation Tips for Kids

1. RECYCLE
Set up three large containers in your home or classroom. Throw away plastic bottles in one, aluminum cans in another and paper (including newspapers) in the third. When the containers are full, ask a grown-up to help you recycle them.

2. PICK UP LITTER
Find and throw away at least three pieces of litter every day. But never grab anything sharp or pointy. Ask a grown-up for help with broken glass and litter that might cause a cut.

3. SAVE WATER
Turn off the faucet as you brush your teeth. Turn on the water only when it's time to rinse.

4. SHUT OFF LIGHTS
When you leave a room, turn off the lights (unless you are coming right back). Also shut off computers, TVs and video games when you are finished with them.

5. KEEP THE REFRIGERATOR DOOR CLOSED
Open the refrigerator only when you know what you need. Grab the item and quickly close the door again.